I0639516

F. Berger Moran

Miss Washington, of Virginia

A Semi-Centennial Love-Story

F. Berger Moran

Miss Washington, of Virginia
A Semi-Centennial Love-Story

ISBN/EAN: 9783743400139

Manufactured in Europe, USA, Canada, Australia, Japa

Cover: Foto ©Andreas Hilbeck / pixelio.de

Manufactured and distributed by brebook publishing software
(www.brebook.com)

F. Berger Moran

Miss Washington, of Virginia

MISS WASHINGTON,

OF VIRGINIA.

A SEMI-CENTENNIAL LOVE-STORY.

BY

MRS. F. BERGER MORAN

Née

JEANNIE BLACKBURN.

FIRST EDITION PUBLISHED FOR THE CENTENNIAL
IN 1889.

ILLUSTRATED.

PHILADELPHIA:
PRESS OF J. B. LIPPINCOTT COMPANY.
1893.

Dedicated

TO

MY DEAR NEPHEW,

BUSHROD C. WASHINGTON,

OF CLAYMONT.

MOUNT VERNON.

The home of Mrs. Judge Bushrod Washington, the great-aunt of the author of this volume.

PREFACE.

THIS little story, which the author desires to place in the hands of every visitor to the World's Fair, was written by the great-granddaughter of Colonel Blackburn, aide-de-camp to Washington during the Revolutionary War. Colonel Blackburn's daughter Annie married Judge Washington. His nephews married her nieces, and one of them—Jane Blackburn—was owner of Mount Vernon and mother of John Augustine Washington, who owned Mount Vernon until it passed into the hands of the Association of Women. Again, the two sisters of the author married the great-great-nephews of General Washington. This near connection enables the writer to give an accurate account of the manners and customs of the family fifty years ago.

The romance is founded on fact, with characters true to name. Even "Mammy Aggy," long since gone to rest, will be recognized by many still living.

———

This popular booklet has been presented to the Society of the Daughters of the American Revolution, together with a large contribution towards its publication, by Mrs. F. Berger Moran, *née* Jeannie Blackburn. All funds arising from the sales at the World's Fair and elsewhere will be donated to the building of a Memorial Hall at Washington for the Sons and Daughters of the American Revolution.

The first one hundred copies will be sold from the table of the Daughters of the American Revolution by Miss Floride Cunningham, the distinguished niece of Miss Pamela Cunningham, the first regent of the Ladies' Mount Vernon Association, for the benefit of the Mount Vernon Home, at the World's Fair.

JEANNIE BLACKBURN.

CHARLOTTESVILLE, VA.

MRS. FANNY LEVY.
Mistress of Monticello.

In Memoriam.

Fanny Mitchell Levy.

JEFFERSON M. LEVY, of Monticello, Virginia, contributed largely towards the publication of this little World's Fair souvenir, in memory of his beloved mother, Mrs. Fanny Mitchell Levy, who died recently at her city residence, in the city of New York. Mrs. Levy was an admirer of the little Virginia story and of its authoress, Mrs. F. Berger Moran.

She was widely known as the charming hostess of Monticello, and will always be remembered as a lovely woman, cordial in her manner, giving genuine, kind welcome to Monticello, taking great pleasure in showing the beauties of the old home to all her guests, and taking great care to have Monticello kept in the colonial style of the days of Jefferson. Mrs. Levy entertained many visitors at this grand old homestead, among them many prominent personages.

In 1888 President Cleveland and some of his
cabinet were her guests.   On October 12, 1892,
she, with her son, received and entertained the
Albemarle Chapter of the Daughters of the
American Revolution, founded by Mrs. F. Berger Moran.   The ball then given was one of the
grandest society events in the history of Virginia, and enabled the regent, Mrs. F. Berger
Moran, to present the first contribution towards
the erection of a Memorial Hall in Washington
for the Daughters of the American Revolution ;
also the first contribution towards the Virginia
Historical Society from any Chapter in the State.
Virginia has lost a good friend in Fanny Mitchell
Levy, Monticello a cherished mistress, and her
children a mother who can never be replaced.

MONTICELLO.
The home of Thomas Jefferson.

CONTENTS.

11

Miss Washington, of Virginia.

2   13

COMYN HALL, CHARLOTTESVILLE, VIRGINIA.

The home of Mrs. F. Berger Moran, the author of this volume.

CHAPTER I.

CUPID IN GERM.

I⊤ was a beautiful night in early June, some fifty years ago, and the ancestral home of the Washingtons was resplendent with light from top to bottom. It was a magnificent building,—with its twenty-three rooms under one roof,—which enabled these elegant people to entertain with the lavish hospitality for which they were so famed. Far away to the front stretched the wooded park, while here and there the harvest-moon was peeping into the faces of the young couples who were making love beneath the shelter of the great oaks. Some extraordinary event was waking the quiet people out of their usual calm. The negroes were all excitement. The house-servants in their crimson linseys, large

15

aprons, white capes, and the red bandan-
nas wound about the head in their own
grotesque style, were nervously flitting
before the windows, or talking in groups
about the "grand doin's"; while the
"quarter negroes" were allowed to press
their black faces against the back window-
panes to see "the white folks dance."

Mr. and Mrs. Washington were cele-
brating the eighteenth birthday of their
only daughter, in the old, regal, Virginia
style.

Pretty young cousins stood in clusters
on the grass circle, whispering and laughing together. Stately dames, with their
modest apparel and refined manners, were
grouped on the portico, discussing Washington Irving's last literary effort, and re-
gretting his prolonged visit to England;
while gray-haired gentlemen were indulg-
ing in heated political discussions.

"I tell you," said Colonel Blackburn,
while his gray eyes beamed with excitement, "I'm an 'old-line Whig,' and I'm

glad of it! The Democratic party is not going to rest content until they destroy this grand old Republic, for which our fathers fought so gallantly."

"Oh, no!" replied Governor Frank J. Thomas, of Maryland, a man of magnificent physique and wonderful brain-power. "We are going to make the grandest nation on the face of the earth! We offer an asylum for the poor and oppressed of all lands. We want muscle to build up our waste places, and, in return, we propose to kindle a spark of manhood in their darkened souls, by giving them a voice in the government under which they live."

"Yes," replied the old colonel, who had fought so hard for the freedom of these United States, "all the nations of the earth will empty their convicts, paupers, and idlers upon the soil of this great country, and I prophesy that one hundred years hence the United States government will be controlled by the vote of the Irish, German, Spanish, Italian, and all others on God's earth, rather than by the American people!"

As the conversation was warming up too much, it was suggested by the mild-mannered host that the gentlemen should imbibe a little whiskey-and-water, which was always set out on the old-fashioned sideboard in the dining-rooms of these Virginia homesteads, and rarely partaken of too freely by the gentlemen.

In the mean while quite a stir was created by "Mammy Aggy," who rushed into the parlor, clapping her hands and exclaiming, with delight, "De Mount Vernon carriage cumin', mistis! cumin' up ter der front do'; I knowed Miss Jane gwyne to make out to git here to-night sure! En here she be!"

Young and old rushed pell-mell, and without ceremony, to welcome the Mount Vernon people. The horses, wearied out with their long journey, dragged themselves around the circle and at last

HARRIS-E

"The horses, wearied out with their long journey, dragged themselves around the circle."

See page 18.

stopped in front of the marble portico of Claymont. A slender, dignified lady emerged from the coach, accompanied by her three handsome children and a maid-servant, Dinah.

"I'm so glad you've got here at last, Aunt Jane; it wouldn't have been a frolic without you," said Marie, as she gave her a warm kiss of welcome.

"Well, Uncle Ben," said Mr. Washington, turning to the old driver, when things had quieted down a little, "you've had a pretty tough time getting here to-night, judging from the looks of your horses."

"Yes, sar; we got inter one ob dem ruts t'other side ob town, and I 'clar I thought Mistis would have ter spend de night dere!"

Then he gave a regular negro laugh, and drove away to take care of his tired beasts.

In a little while the young folks established Jess and Joss, the negro fiddler and bone-player, in one corner of the back parlor, and secured partners for the cotillon.

The merriment was at its height when Cousin Lee Turner was announced, the only son of Mr. Washington's sister. The dance stopped for a few moments while Cousin Lee formally introduced his friend and college chum, Mr. Allan Cadwallader, of Philadelphia, to the bevy of pretty girls about him.

While Allan was engaged in a charming chat with one of the ladies he was struck with the unusual beauty of the young girl conversing so animatedly with Lee, and begged to know " who she was."

" Why, that is Marie," replied his companion. " The ball is given in her honor. She is eighteen to-night. Have you not been presented ?"

" Not yet," he replied.

" How negligent ! Give me the pleasure."

Allan offered his arm gallantly, and

they were soon in the presence of the two
earnest talkers.

"Allow me to present Mr. Cadwallader, Miss Washington."

Lee looked a little annoyed at the in-
terruption, and Allan's companion became quite jealous of the all-devouring
attention he paid the débutante.

Allan was a complete man of the world,
versed in all its cunning and coquetry,
but he stood somewhat abashed in the
presence of so much delicate loveliness.

A tall, shapely, but girlish figure, a
stately poise of the head, large, hazel
eyes shot with red lights, brown hair of
golden tinge, an olive complexion, and
bright color, slightly retroussé nose, and
a cunning rose-bud mouth, completed the
picture of Miss Washington at eighteen.

It did not take Allan long to find that
his friend, Lee Turner, was infatuated
with this beautiful cousin, and could
hardly believe him to be the same quiet
man who rode by his side a few moments

since, discussing the merits of old Virginia customs, and recalling happy scenes in their college-life. The burning eyes, flushed face, and stammering tongue all bore evidence of some unusual emotion which was stirring this noble heart to its depth.

Now, no man likes to see another man claim possession of a beautiful woman. There is a great deal of the animal in man's nature. Like the dog, he only fights for the bone that another dog wants.

The quiet air of possession assumed by Lee, when he claimed her hand for the first quadrille, seemed to arouse in Allan a spirit of rivalry; for during the pause in the music which preceded the dance, he found himself, instead of seeking another partner, bringing all his fascination of person, mind, and manners to bear upon this attractive Southern girl.

Marie had the brilliancy of a Ninon de l'Enclos, strangely combined with a native reserve. In her conversation gushes of wit and merriment, sparkling humor, and quaint satire followed each other in quick succession, mingled with a dignity which made her irresistible.

Allan was completely intoxicated, and requested the honor of the second quadrille. Afterwards he found himself promenading on the wide back portico, with the moonlight touching up Marie's high-bred features, and shining on the marble arm which rested within his own.

They talked of "Cousin Lee," and Allan told her that, although Lee was a good many years younger than himself, he had always been unaccountably drawn towards a nature so unique and grand.

"Now, I shall have to thank him all my life," he said, earnestly, "for this glimpse into your Arcadian life."

"It is odd you should be such a friend of Cousin Lee's," replied Marie, taking a modest side-glance at her companion, " because you are so very different."

"May I ask in what way?"

"Oh, I hardly know," she replied, ringing out a hearty laugh; "Lee is one of the best of men, and I fancy—she hesitated a moment, and then laughingly added—you have a little *diablerie* hidden in your nature."

"Now, don't you think you are quite harsh in your judgment of me?"

Here Allan pretended to be very much wounded, and said, after a few moments of silence, "What a different opinion I have formed of your ladyship."

"Now do tell me," urged Marie, "what you think of me."

"It is that you are so different from all these great-aunts and cousins who surround you. In fact," he whispered, as another claimed her hand for the dance, "I have found a sparkling diamond in a setting of pearls."

Marie crimsoned; it was so nice to be appreciated so highly.

In a little while Allan found himself

pressing nearer the circle of young men who hung around Marie, and urging another promenade on the piazza. It was granted.

" Just think," said Allan, as he seated Marie at the upper end of the portico, where the moonlight brought out her statuesque beauty, and threw himself on a divan at her feet, " what a change from my dusty banking-house to this scene of wonderful beauty, music, flowers, dancing;—and the great-niece of the 'father of our country' to rouse my senses into a dangerous activity."

Then Mammy Aggy approached with a waiter bearing two tumblers and a cut-glass decanter filled with the far-famed home-made currant-wine, so much used in those old Virginia households.

" Miss Marie," she urged, in her fond freedom, " what is you settin' out here widdout nothin' on yer head? Don't you know yer par and mar would go clean 'stracted ef yer was to catch cold?"

"Oh, mammy, do let me alone," Marie replied, in a childish tone, "on my birthday.

"I will go in," she said, in obedience to an ominous shake of mammy's head, "if you will send us Nip and Tuck (mammy's grandsons) to dance for Mr. Cadwallader."

Of course, mammy complied with her request immediately, and they were soon looking on at the heel-and-toe dance of these remarkable twins. They were of exactly the same height, with the same ebony skin, broad, hanging lips, and large, black eyes, rolling in their sockets. They performed their grotesque jigs without a change of expression, amid the laughter and encouragement of the by-standers. Then Miss Washington stepped forward and presented each with a handsome gift, in memory of her birthday. In some way Marie's bracelet became entangled in the muslin of her dress, loosened its fastening, and fell to

They performed their grotesque jigs without a change of expression.

See page 26.

the floor. Allan picked it up quickly, and stooped to fasten it on her arm.

What an unconscionable time it took him to fasten that bracelet! He noted the round, shapely, white arm; the long, slender hand, with its tapering fingers and rosy nails. "An artist's arm," he observed with a smile, as Miss Washington impatiently withdrew it.

Then there was the hospitable supper and the Old-Virginia reel, in which all the stately couples joined, and the merriment waxed greater as the hours flew by. At last twelve o'clock struck from the tall clock in the corner, and the guests departed.

CHAPTER II.

THE BIRTHDAY OF THE GOD OF LOVE.

As Lee and Allan rode back to Wheatland they were strangely quiet. Allan was pondering in his mind whether it was possible he was falling in love with this pretty Virginia girl. "What folly!" and his mind wandered away to the many flirtations he had had with beautiful women, more or less spicy, involving some little intrigue, and always attended with more or less pleasure. He excused himself, as he knocked the ashes from his cigar, by saying to himself, "They were old dissemblers in the art of playing at love. Bah!" he thought, with a shrug of his shoulders, "it never hurt them. But this winsome Virginia girl! Of course, I never intend to marry at all. Then what's the use of spoiling

28

Lee's life? He is a noble fellow and would make her a very excellent husband."

For some reason he did not fancy this picture. "She will develop into a grand woman some day," he thought, gravely, "when experience takes the baby-lights out of her superbly innocent eyes. Jove! what a pleasure it would be to teach her to love!"

He *fancied* this picture, and dwelt on it until they rode up and dismounted at Wheatland.

For many days Allan and Lee were frequent visitors at Claymont,—the former always managing to draw Marie out of the crowd, under the shade of the old oaks, or wandering with her through the gardens and shrubbery, dallying on the banks of the little lake which lay at the foot of the lawn, or cantering through the country on their handsome horses.

He would hold frequent converse with his conscience. " Delicious, very delicious," he would say at these times, " but cannot last. I have never been really in love,—that is, had my passions stirred to their depths. I shall go back to the city and forget this bewitching siren. I defy any one to tell whether that proud creature cares a rush for me. Sometimes I am quite sure of it; a blush, a glance, a hesitating, trembling manner will reveal her heart to me. If I presume on my knowledge, how quickly my lady puts me in the rightful place again. To-morrow I will find out whether she is *betrothed* to Lee."

The sun rose bright and clear the next morning, and found the party of young people *en route* for Shanondale Springs, where they were going to hold a picnic. Of course Allan had Marie as his companion on the trip.

As they cantered along briskly, feeling the exhilarating influence of the crisp morning air, the bright sunshine, the singing birds, and their near proximity to each other, Allan exclaimed, as he looked on her mass of brown tresses, which had been shaken out of a demure knot in their wild canter, and now lay in disorder on her shoulders,—

"How I wish I could gather the sunlight on those tresses and carry it back with me to my bachelor-home in the city. Just think how dreary and lonely I will be after this wild holiday!"

Marie answered, hurriedly, "Oh! I imagine no one gets lonesome in a great city. You'll soon forget us all and settle down quite naturally in your old quarters."

He thought he discovered a certain tremor in her voice, and hastened on.

"Of course, you will forget all about *me*," he said, quivering with excitement; "but I will carry away into my lonely future the beautiful picture of a brown-eyed Southern girl, which will torment me for many long hours."

Marie raised her curling lashes with a half-startled expression, and wondered what was coming into her life. A blush of shame mounted up into the face of this worldling.

"So much innocence!" he thought,— and for a moment he hesitated. "Shall I tempt her? Shall I *know* whether she cares?" and reaching forward he touched the hand lying lazily on the pommel of her saddle.

She started like a deer caught in a thicket; but, quickly remembering herself, drew her hand angrily away, and, straightening her regal form, gave Allan such a look of contempt as to confound even this man of the world.

"Does that little hand belong to another, that you guard it so closely?" exclaimed Allan, ferociously.

"Perhaps so," said Marie, as she recovered her former repose of manner; and, reining up her horse, proposed a gallop.

"She is the proudest woman I ever knew," thought Allan. "I wonder if, after all, she *loves* Lee. I will find out."

They stopped to take breath; Marie's rich color and sparkling eyes were making a madman of Allan.

"You are young to be so cruel," he urged. "Here I have been your slave for weeks, and you are less partial to me than at the beginning of our acquaintance. I have almost lost my manhood dallying beneath these Southern skies. Oh, my Ice Queen," he exclaimed, in a hoarse whisper, as he seized her bridle-rein, and, holding it firmly, compelled her to listen to him, "answer me one question and I have done: Do you love that confounded Cousin Lee?"

He stooped for her answer. Every nerve in Marie's body was tingling with excitement, but she answered, with a playful hauteur,—

"Have you any right to ask that question of me?"

One could almost have heard the wild

c

throbs of Allan's heart as he threw prudence to the winds and said, in a quiet, determined voice,—

" The right that any man has to claim any woman as his own who does not belong to another."

The color mounted into Marie's cheek, up into her temples, and was lost amid her brown curls.

" This is sheer nonsense," she said, gayly, as she administered a playful cut of her whip on the hand that held her rein ; " we must overtake our party."

She avoided any further conversation with her lover, and during the whole day showed a marked preference for Cousin Lee's society. And when Cadwallader, in desperation, proposed that she should accompany him in a light canoe which had been launched on the river for the benefit of the picnic party, she smiled and said "she would not think of venturing on the water unless Cousin Lee rowed the boat."

Cadwallader, who had his hand on the oar at the time, dropped it as if he had been struck ; then, springing on shore, gallantly assisted Marie into the boat, and motioned to Lee to remain by her side, while at the same time he whispered,—

"I will leave you to your desired *tête à tête* with Cousin Lee."

"The miserable day is over at last," thought Allan, whose enjoyment had been spoiled by Marie's avoidance of him. For the return homeward he brought her horse up, and, kneeling, held his hand gallantly. She put her pretty plump foot into it, as was the custom in those knightly days, and sprang gracefully into her saddle.

"Thank God! I'm going to have you to myself for a while," he whispered, as Lee, who had come up to see whether the girth of her saddle was tight, walked off with a pleasant " good-night."

The sun was just sinking below the Blue Ridge, touching up with its dying splendor the many-hued cloudlets; the birds were twittering in their nests; even the rivulets had a subdued murmur, as they trickled along over their pebbly beds towards the sea. The road wound in and out among the rich grain-fields, ready for harvest, and sometimes they would canter past handsome old home-steads and remark on their beauty.

For some reason Allan was *distrait*, while Marie chattered on incessantly. He was thinking, " What in the name of all that's holy am I doing,—making love to a child? Bah! pull yourself together again, Allan Cadwallader, and don't you dare trifle with this young girl's heart."

Marie was wondering if the ride would ever come to an end, when Allan said, abruptly,—

" I hope you enjoyed your sail."

" Supremely; the river was so beau-tiful, and Cousin Lee is so strong one never feels afraid of him."

"I'm glad I didn't go; if any difficulty had occurred you might have thrown me overboard."

Marie laughed in her usually happy way, when Allan, with his brows knit and a very solemn expression, asked, "If you were in mid-ocean in a frail boat with Lee and me as companions, and a fearful storm arose in which it was necessary that one of us should leap out to save the lives of the other two, which would you let sink out of your sight forever?"

His face was flushed, his eyes fastened on her proud face with intense eagerness.

"Virginians always stand by their cousins," she said, playfully.

He was downright angry now. "Was this child trying to play with him?" he thought, savagely, "or was she in love and struggling with her pride to hide it from him?"

Of course he was vain enough to believe the latter.

447981

"I *will* find out," he thought, triumphantly.

"You have more soul than any woman I ever met, Miss Washington, and I'm tempted to confide a little love-story to your ears."

"Do tell me!" exclaimed Marie, catching the earnest tone of the speaker.

"Once upon a time there grew in a king's garden a delicate white violet, which had disengaged itself from the parent bed. Near it the gardener transplanted a shapely rose-tree from a northern clime. The rose-tree was ambitious, and shot up its green arms towards the sunlight, opening its delicate leaves to the laughing showers, forgetting all the while that a dangerous canker was gnawing at its exposed root. It bore no flowers. The violet did not seem to thrive, either, because its young leaves were beaten by the tempest and scorched by the rays of the sun."

Marie was restless under his searching glance.

"The rose-tree became enamoured of the modest violet, but knowing its unworthiness, it moralized thus: 'I have been a long time in this garden, and in spite of the pruning-knife, the sunshine and showers, I make no progress towards strength or beauty; while my great arms are filled with naughty briers, so that I dare not embrace the modest violet. Each day she seems to grow away from me, afraid of my cruel kisses.' A gust of wind carried the cry of the disconsolate rose-tree, 'What shall I do? Oh! what shall I do?' A gentle zephyr swept over the modest violet's bed, and whispered to the despairing rose-tree, 'I would come to you, beloved, if I dared,—if I dared; but all around about me urges me to cling to my native soil and the parental home. What shall I do? Oh! what shall I do?'"

Marie looked away affrighted. Allan had been talking so quietly, the rein lying idly on his horse's neck, while his whole face was illumined with a strange light.

Marie, desperately interested, and impatient at his long silence, said, breathlessly,—

"Well?"

"Ah!" he exclaimed, triumphantly, "thank God! it was 'well,' at last. A terrible storm came, and with its mighty power tore up the modest violet and cast it near the trunk of the enamoured rose-tree. It stooped from its lofty height, spread its strong arms around about the violet, sheltering it from the storm and the sun's rays, until it was firmly rooted at the base of the rose-tree's trunk, when it not only bloomed more beautifully than ever, but nestled by the beautiful bush, until one day the gardener exclaimed, 'Behold, my rose-tree in full bloom!' The approach of the violet, and the perfume which it exhaled, had remedied all all evils."

They had reached the portico and dismounted, when Allan whispered,—

"Oh, that I may be the pining rose-tree, whose first bloom was brought out by the clinging tenderness of *my modest violet!*"

Marie struggled to disengage the hand which he held in his own as in a vise, while her face was suffused with burning blushes.

"Let me go. Oh! please let me go!" she pleaded; "I'm not well, indeed I'm not, and will keep my room for to-night. Good-by."

He released her hand.

"She flies! She's mine," mused Allan, triumphantly, as he rode away, "*if* I want her. Do I? That is the question."

CHAPTER III.

CUPID SPREADS HIS WINGS.

On Allan's return to Wheatland he found Lee Turner slowly promenading up and down the length of the portico, evidently busied with grave thoughts, so much so that he only nodded to Allan, called the servant to take his guest's horse, and then, folding his hands behind him again, proceeded with his solemn tramp.

"Cousin Lee is jealous," thought Allan, who felt sure something unusual was stirring the depths of this loyal nature: "I will give him a chance to speak." Tilting his chair against the wall, he coolly lit his cigar, and began,—

"Well, old fellow, father is anxious to have his good-for-nothing son back again, and I must go to-morrow."

Lee halted for a moment, and a heavy frown contracted his handsome brow, succeeded by a more genial expression when he remembered his relation of host.

"Is not your determination rather sudden?" he said, still struggling to control his turbulent feelings; "have you said anything to Marie about it?" His voice trembled when he called her name.

"Oh! you can say to her how sorry I was to go without telling her good-by," he replied, carelessly knocking the ashes from his cigar by touching it lightly on the arm of his chair.

"Let's walk out on the lawn a little way," said Lee, with suppressed emotion. "I have something to say to you, Allan."

Allan arose quickly, and accompanied him, somewhat surprised at the strange manner of his companion. Lee offered his friend a garden-chair, and stood in front of him.

"Dear Allan," he began, "you and I have loved and respected each other for a long time. I want nothing to come between us to mar the beauty of our early friendship."

"Of course not," said Allan, awkwardly.

"Then we must keep no secrets from each other. It is no news to you, my dear fellow, that I have always loved Marie."

"This is a strange fellow," thought Allan; "what is he blundering into? I suppose he is going to tell me not to steal his property. Egad! I was tempted to leave her to him; now I'll fight for her."

Lee hesitated and went on: "Loved her since my earliest boyhood. It has been admitted by both families that we are intended for one another, and it has been no secret kept from either of us. I would have told her how devotedly I loved her, but I have been deterred by her evident dislike to the subject."

Allan was now making a psychological study of this noble specimen of the human race.

" If you love her, God bless her;" and he lifted his hat from his head
reverently.

See page 45.

" And I wanted to say to you," he continued, with a remarkable effort at self-control, " that if you love her, God bless her," and he lifted his hat from his head reverently and proceeded with difficulty, " and want to make her your bride, I will not stand in your way. That is all."

Allan was peculiarly constituted. So long as there were obstacles in his way to fight, he was quite sure he was deeply enough in love with Miss Washington to give up even his club-life and all that bachelors hold dear ; but now, when she seemed " thrown at his head," as it were, he was very certain that he did not want to marry *any one*.

Oh, the perversity of man's nature !

" What a grand old fellow you are !" exclaimed Allan, springing from his chair and grasping his friend's hand. " It's altogether a mistake, and your sacrifice is not required. Miss Washington and I are friends only."

" You don't mean to say," cried Lee,

dropping Allan's hand in disgust, " that you are daring to trifle with this young girl's heart; that you have robbed me of my sweetheart, and Marie of her peace of mind! My God! I will not believe it of you."

He stood like an avenging angel, his hand uplifted as though to strike, when suddenly he fell to the ground in a deep swoon.

Allan rushed to the house for assistance, and the devoted parents were soon using every remedy to restore their only son.

He found it was no unusual thing for Lee to have these death-like swoons when under any excitement. The doctors had feared some valvular affection of the heart.

It was some time before Lee became quite himself again. Then Allan whispered, " I will tell you all presently. I am not as base as you think."

They were called in to partake of one

of those delicious " Virginia suppers,"— beaten biscuits, dripped coffee, butter fresh from the churn, with flannel-cakes, birds, etc.

It gave one a glorious appetite just to look at the nicely-appointed table ; but the royal hospitality, the genial cheer, the sparkling wit, helped one also to digest.

Allan retired early.

" I will not risk another conversation to-night," he thought ; but when he had closed his door, and drew the *stiff-backed "easy-chair"* towards the window, he threw himself into it lazily, and, crossing his feet on the broad window-sill, prepared to interview his heart.

" It is clear," thought he, " that I will have to make up my mind whether or not I love and am prepared to marry Miss Washington. Lee is the noblest fellow God ever made ! How like a prince he bade me woo the woman for whom he would die ! Not the men I've been accustomed to meet in this selfish world. She thinks she loves me. Poor girl, if she only knew how unlike I am to her noble cousin,—not worthy to draw off his boot. Egad! why don't she love him? If I were a woman I would worship such a man. I would be proud to be called by his name, honored by his companionship. It is the first woman I ever met who disturbed my whole being! This point I must admit."

Then he puffed away at his cigar, and thought dreamily of the fawn-like eyes, the statuesque neck, bust, and arms, the magnificent carriage, and the noble birth of Miss Washington. He compared her with the women who had tempted him into follies in the past.

There was the beautiful Clara Lovemoney, who had sought after and flattered him into a boyish infatuation, until he heard she had consulted a lawyer with regard to the amount of his marriage portion from his rich parent. Then he had turned from her with disgust, and sought only to while away a leisure hour with the fair sex.

How grandly this girl's picture stood out from the rest! Her nobility of heart, shown in every expression of her mobile features, her purity, modesty, refinement, her sparkling wit, her brilliancy in conversation!

Then he thought of the grand old couple who had reared this beautiful flower, only to keep it near them in their own garden. She was worthy of Lee, and Lee was worthy of her. Why not leave them to their own Eden? They would work out the problem of their own happiness by living for each other. The child would forget him, he thought, sadly, much sooner than he would forget her.

Allan had some noble traits of character mixed up with his worldly nature, and would have been a different man had not his faith in women been paralyzed in early manhood.

He had wealth, position, beauty of person, and a powerful intellect,—was, indeed, a splendid fiancé for any woman; but he had grown cynical, blasé, and world-weary at twenty-eight years of age. He had seen so many of his club-mates infatuated with women, wedded to their angels, only to find them intensely human,—often uncongenial and false.

"He would steer clear of matrimony," he thought, "at any rate."

Then the blushing face of his "modest violet" would inflame his imagination, and tempt him into a dream-land dangerous to his peace of mind.

The sunlight stole in at the open casement and waked him from his delirium.

He dared not stay another day, and as he rode by the side of his companion towards the town where he was to take the train, he assured him that no word of love had ever passed between Miss Washington and himself. He admitted his admiration for her, and spoke of her graces of mind and body in eloquent terms; but told him that in the absence of any encouragement he had withdrawn his suit.

He sent kindly adieux to Claymont, and regretted his hurried return to his father's banking-house.

When they parted he seized Lee's hand, and, looking earnestly into his face, exclaimed,—

"God bless you, old fellow! Let us always be friends."

"Remember, Allan," said the Virginian, in a husky voice, "I want no favors: I will have only what belongs to me. If Marie loves you, you only have a right to her hand. Let there be no trifling anywhere now."

"I assure you," said Allan, earnestly, "you are making a mountain out of a mole-hill."

The whistle shrieked, and as he hastened up the steps of the platform he whispered, "I shall yet dance at your wedding," and was off to the city again.

CHAPTER IV.

THERE was a startling change in Marie after Allan's departure. She grew pale and listless, wandering alone among her flowers, or writing poetry out on the old stile where she and Allan had so often sat together, or listening, down on the lake-side, to the wild concert of birds which made the woods ring with their melody.

There was only one time in the day that her lethargy would be followed by renewed activity,—the hour for the northern mail. She would mount her horse then and plunge into the town herself, not waiting for the colored boy to do his errand, only to meet with continued disappointment.

"Ah," she would muse at such times,

"if he could leave me without saying good-by, then he never loved me, and I was so weak as to let him lead me captive at his will."

If there was one trait more developed than another in this young girl it was her pride.

"He dared to trifle with me," she thought, wildly, "and I have nothing to do but to keep my cruel secret. I gave him, unasked, it is true, a heart he did not want, and he played with it until he sent the life-blood into my tell-tale face, and then he left me forever; what shall I do! Oh, what shall I do!"

She would one day avoid Lee; the next be overwhelmed with joy to see him.

The poor fellow thought her vacillating, weak, perhaps feverish.

One day in the early spring, two years after the departure of Allan, Marie ventured to question her cousin concerning him.

"Do you ever hear from your old friend, Allan Cadwallader?"

She put her question so indifferently, and without a change in voice or face, that Lee felt convinced now that she did not care for Allan as he had feared, and answered by taking from his coat-pocket a letter just received, and reading its contents aloud.

Allan spoke in glowing terms of his success in business, his father's delight at his unusual activity, and his urgent desire that his friend should visit him at an early date; then he dropped into this bit of news,—

"You will remember my old love-affair with Clara Lovemoney. Well, her rich husband met with an accident some time ago in the Alps and was killed; so she is a rich and fascinating widow. Who knows but your humble servant may be again at her feet?"

Not a muscle of Marie's face moved. How this child-woman could teach even her heart's blood not to flush into her face was a secret, but she did it.

She laughed merrily and exclaimed,—

"Think of him married to a widow! Won't she rehash all her old 'curtain lectures,' and craze and worry him out of his habitual good humor?"

"I do not think it means anything serious," said Lee, as he refolded the letter gravely and replaced it in his pocket. "I always thought Allan cared more for you, Marie, than any other woman."

She was not prepared for this outburst, and, recovering from her confusion, with another forced laugh, said,—

"As you have undertaken to do your friend's courting, I must tell you that I thoroughly dislike him, and that you are entirely mistaken in regard to his feeling towards me."

Marie became playful, bright, fascinating; something had awakened a "daredevil" spirit in the young girl now.

"She certainly did not care for Allan,"

thought Lee; "then why should she not care for him?"

They were wandering by the side of the lake now. The sun was just dropping behind the mountain-tops, reflecting its rays in the clear water at their feet, while the freshly-opening leaves and newly-springing grass were stirred by the evening breeze.

Wearied with her walk and the prolonged effort at self-control, Marie threw herself in a garden-chair, and loosening the comb from her hair, let it fall in rich luxuriance over her shoulders.

Lee stood for a moment contemplating her wonderful beauty. The dying sunlight played about her dimpled mouth, danced amid her golden tresses, and kissed her white brow. Why should not he?

"Marie," he exclaimed, throwing himself wildly at her feet, "I have loved you all my life! If you do not love Allan, why not love me?"

" Which shall it be ?"

See page 57.

He seized her hand and was about to print a mad kiss upon it, when she drew it away angrily, and said, with her native hauteur returning,—

"Please don't do anything so silly, Cousin Lee; if you will take this seat," pointing to a chair near by, "I will listen to what you have to say."

Poor Lee was so confounded by this rebuff that he hardly knew how to proceed, but told her in a stammering voice, choked by emotion, how many years he had loved her; how often he would have thrown himself at her feet, but feared her heart was Allan's, and dared not; how he had taken courage at last, when she said she did not care for him at all.

"And now, Marie," he implored, "send me away a broken, ruined man, or your betrothed husband. Which shall it be?"

He was leaning towards her chair, looking into her eyes with all the intense passion of a man roused into life.

Marie was strangely cold and silent for a time; then, rousing herself, she said, quietly,—

"I don't think I am capable of loving anybody much, but, if you want me to love you as mamma loves papa,—in a quiet, elegant way,—I might teach myself to do it. I had thought I was going to be different from that when I married, but—but," she stammered and looked away towards the setting sun, "if you want me, and think you would be satisfied with that kind of love, and—and don't forget yourself as you did just now, I will marry you."

Lee sprang to his feet indignantly, and exclaimed,—

"Are you a woman playing with my passion thus for pastime, or are you a child, not knowing whither your feet are straying? If you do not love me, Marie, I do not want you for my wife."

Marie's face flushed an angry crimson,

and then she burst into tears. "Forgive me," she cried, "if I wounded you. I did not mean to. You are a noble fellow, and I will love you as you deserve." ˑ

Lee was as gentle as a woman now; blaming himself for wounding her feelings, calling himself a "high-strung brute," and telling her, "she should never repent her choice."

"I might have known," he said, trying to laugh her tears away, "that no young girl would like her lover to rush at her like a great bear. I will try to be more like 'papa;'" and he threw his head back and laughed heartily.

Then he wandered towards the house with Marie on his arm, so proud of his betrothed bride.

But there was a voice crying out in Marie's soul that refused to be stifled.

"Why let your wounded pride," it cried, "drive you to such a mad act? Why be false to your woman's nature?

Why ruin his life, too?" She tried to
quiet it by saying to herself,—

"I will make him such a good wife—
such a good wife."

CHAPTER V.

CUPID HITS THE MARK WITH HIS GOLDEN ARROW.

THERE was great delight in both families when their engagement was announced, and it was touching to see the wild joy of the old family negroes at the approach of the " big wedding," which was to take place in early June.

Mammy Aggy was the only one who did not seem to enter into the joy of the rest; and so, one night when Marie was having her beautiful hair combed out by Mammy, she said, inquiringly,—

"You don't seem to be happy, Mammy?"

" What I gwine ter be happy 'bout, chile, when Solmun worritin' my life out 'bout gwine 'way wid yer ?"

"Oh ! mammy !" exclaimed Marie, joyfully, "are you going with me to Wheat-land?"

"In course I is, chile. Did yer 'spect I were gwine ter leave you when I dun nussed yer at dis old black breas'? I ar'n't never gwine ter leave yer; but I 'fesses when I thinks of leavin' poor old master and mistis"—here the tears coursed down Mammy's black, shiny face —"I does git kinder upsot. I says to Solmun las' night—says I, 'Solmun, you and me is mity fond ob one anudder, but we 'bleeged to part. Dat chile can't do widout her old mammy; and yer aint so old dat yer can't make out ter walk over to Mars' Lee's once in er while.' But he looked like he pouted wus 'en ever at dat; den I told him, 'pintedly, 'I'm gwine.'"

Mammy laid down the brush and, coming in front of Marie, repeated, gesticulating violently with both arms, "I'm gwine; dat's all dere is 'bout it."

Marie seized her old black mammy

and kissed her face, as she delighted to do when a child ; then, flinging herself on the bed, burst into a passion of tears, exclaiming,—

"Oh, mammy! mammy! Do you think I will be happy?"

"Why, what's de marter wid yer, chile?" exclaimed the old negro, aghast at this spectacle. "Ob course yer gwine ter be happy wid Mars' Lee! Ain't he 'stracted in love wid yer? He think more ob one ob de stones under your feet 'en he do ob de whole heaven! What's de marter wid yer, den? Yer'll git all rite arter it's ober."

After a few more comforting expressions like these, Mammy tidied up the room and tucked Marie cosily in her bed, as she had done every night since her birth.

The next morning Marie announced her intention of paying a long-promised visit to her friend Miss Cox, in Philadelphia. It did not occasion much surprise in the family, as she was going somewhere to arrange about her *trousseau* for the coming wedding.

She was courted, fêted, wined, and dined in the Quaker City by all the leading families, but kept the secret of her approaching marriage locked up in her own heart. She had seen Allan nowhere in all these gay crowds. She dared not raise her eyes in the opera-house or the theatre lest they should rest on his face.

"What shall I do if I meet him? What shall I do if I don't?" was her daily cry.

At last, one night at a great ball given by one of Miss Cox's friends, Allan Cadwallader was standing near the door talking to a flashily-dressed woman, when Miss Washington entered. Marie had changed greatly: all her old-time beauty lingered, it was true, with the addition of a superbly-developed figure, and the soul-light in her large brown eyes that experience alone can kindle. She was dressed in a superb crimson brocade train, with " bertha" of point lace falling gracefully away from her superb neck, and exposing her rounded arms. She wore several strings of pearls around her neck and about her shapely wrists,—the family jewels. Crimson fuchsias decorated her dress and shone amid the coils of her brown hair.

" What a magnificent woman !" exclaimed Allan to his companion when their eyes met.

Marie looked away quickly to recover her wonted self-possession, while Allan begged to be excused; he must speak to this lady, " who was a very dear friend."

Marie was busily chatting with her many admirers when Allan broke the circle and pressed to her side.

" This is, indeed, a great pleasure, Miss Washington," he exclaimed, his whole face beaming with the joy he expe-

rienced ; " I had not heard of your ar-
rival."

" A shocking admission, Cadwallader,"
laughed one of her many admirers, " of
your own obscurity, as Miss Washington
has been the toast and belle here for over
two weeks."

Marie laughed heartily at the discom-
fiture of her old friend, and chatted away
brilliantly to the crowd about her.

Allan stood and feasted his eyes upon
the matured beauty of the girl-woman he
had left among her hills so long a time
ago.

" Do you waltz, now, Miss Washington ?" he inquired, as the band struck up
his favorite waltz.

" Oh, yes," she replied, quickly, " papa
and mamma had to yield the point. I
got so mortally tired of dancing with only
cousins"—here she arched her eyebrows
coquettishly, shrugged her white shoulders, and proceeded, with a pretty pout—
" I have always been so fearfully spoilt,

you know, by those dear parents of mine."

"Give me a waltz," urged Allan.

"I think you are too late," she said, cruelly, surveying her full card. *Au revoir,*" and she went off in the arms of another man before his very eyes.

Allan stood and watched her slow, graceful, swan-like movements.

"She does not love her Cousin Lee," he thought, joyfully; "I have given him two years and he has made no progress. I will try for the prize myself."

Now, Allan was trying to convince himself that generosity towards his friend alone prompted him to leave the ripe fruit which he ought to have gathered, and so strong was this conviction taking hold of him that even now his restless conscience whispered,—

"You have given your word to Lee, as a gentleman, that you would not interfere with his suit; then why this madness?"

No man can stand the temptation that

forbidden fruit presents; and then Satan whispered into the listening ear,—

"You are making a fool of yourself! Why not find out whether she *cared* when you left her so cruelly, or whether *she*, too, was playing a game for her own amusement; whether this is a vital question at all between you, or she only a heartless coquette?"

"I will plunge in," he said to himself, as he shook off his prolonged reverie, "if I'm drowned."

"Miss Washington," he pleaded, "one waltz for the sake of 'auld lang syne.'"

"I am very tired,"—she hesitated a moment,—"but I will give it to you. Do you manage everybody as easily as you do me?" ("Oh, God! had she said too much?") And again the hot blood flushed into her cheek and dyed the whiteness of her brow.

Allan, seeing this surging of emotion, could not trust himself to answer; but, trembling with delight, placed his arm about her waist and took her hand in his; he felt her warm breath on his cheek.

"She *shall* be my wife," he thought, triumphantly, " if *she will.*"

" At what hour can I see you to-morrow ? and where are you staying ?" whispered Allan.

" I leave in a week," she replied, "and my hours are all engaged."

"Don't be cruel! I must see you to-morrow at twelve o'clock."

" This is my waltz, Miss Washington ; I cannot have another cheat me out of it," interrupted one of her admirers.

As Allan released his arm from her waist a bunch of crushed fuchsias fell from her dress. He picked them up, glanced at the blood-red spot they had left on the snowy whiteness of her bust, and pinned them in the button-hole of his coat.

On the morrow, Allan dressed himself with unusual care, and, having found out

where Marie was staying, presented himself at the front-door precisely at twelve
o'clock.   In response to the door-bell, a
grave-looking butler appeared.

" Miss Washington in ?"

" No, sir ; she went out early this morning."

" Did she leave no message ?"

" No, sir."

And Allan, very much troubled in
spirit at this positive rebuff, retraced his
steps.

" I will see her again before she leaves,"
he thought, humbly.   " I will follow her
to her home.   She *shall* love me !   She
shall be mine !"

He called again and again ; she was
always out.   He had sought her at the
theatres, in the streets, everywhere,—but
with no success.   At last he was invited
to a ball given at Mr. Cox's, in honor of
Miss Washington, who was to leave for
her home in the morning.

It is hardly necessary to say he went,

much humbled, too, by his bitter experience of the past week, but a more determined lover than ever.

Marie was dressed in white brocade, garnished with lace. On her bust and in her hair lay bunches of pure white violets. The light, airy whiteness of her costume, not touched up anywhere with a ray of color, contrasted wonderfully with the crimson of her lips and cheeks, the rich brown of her hair and eyes, the long, dark lashes, and noble brow. She looked a very queen to-night, and was holding her court when Allan entered. He glanced at her dress, and when he saw "the modest violets" resting on her bosom, in her hair, he could scarcely control himself sufficiently to speak to her.

"You are wearing *my* flowers to-night," he whispered, as he bore her off in triumph on his arm. "You will remember how much I loved them?"

They had entered the conservatory,

and Marie, in answer, plucked a rose from a flourishing rose-tree and pinned it in his coat.

"You will wear *mine*," she said, blushing a scarlet hue.

"Oh, no; 'a fair exchange is no robbery.' Give me my modest violet (he plucked one from her dress), and you may do what you will with the stately rose-tree's bloom."

She threw it on the floor and laughingly stamped her slipper upon it.

"Is he daring to flirt with me again?" thought Marie, with her wounded pride crying out for revenge. "We will see; we will see."

"How cold and cruel you are, Marie!"

Her heart throbbed as though it would burst. How dare he call her by her name? She threw her head back with haughty poise, and waited.

"You know that I love you. Why do you avoid me?"

"Maidens never tell their secrets," she

" Don't you think this comedy has gone far enough ?"

See page 73.

whispered, as another claimed her for his waltz, and bore her away in triumph.

Allan had no chance to speak to her again until he claimed her for his own waltz. Then he said all manner of wild, endearing things, until Marie stopped abruptly and exclaimed, under her breath, "Don't you think this comedy has gone far enough?" There was a blaze of angry passion in the girl's face, quite inexplicable to Allan.

"It may be a comedy to you, Miss Washington, but to me it is the most serious moment in my life. May I go home with you to-morrow?" he urged.

"Not to-morrow," she said, thoughtfully; "but if you are really in earnest," —the crimson of shame dyed her face for the first time in all her life,—"you may come to Claymont next week,"—she hesitated,—"the fifteenth of June."

"Oh, my love! my love!" whispered Allan as they parted, "remember the fifteenth of June."

D 7

CHAPTER VI.

CUPID BRANDISHES A TORCH WITH WHICH HE DESTROYS HIMSELF.

THE fifteenth of June arrived, and Allan, fatigued by his long car-ride, was glad to exchange his seat for one in the comfortable family-carriage which he found waiting for him at the station.

"*She* did not forget," he thought, joyfully, as he accosted old "Uncle Sol."

"Well, Uncle Sol, it's been a long time since I had the pleasure of shaking hands with you."

"Yes, sah!" replied the delighted old negro. "Dat's a fac', sure an' sartin. I surely is glad ter see you back ag'in, marster; do dis makes de second trip I dun took to dis place ter-day. De horses is jest fagged out. 'Tother gemman didn't come; I 'peared at de right time, but he didn't occur."

Allan smiled at the old negro's grotesque English, and was soon rolling towards his beloved.

He pulled out his cigar-case, took from it a cigar, lit it, and lay back in the luxurious carriage.

It was a still night, not a sound to be heard but the rattling of the carriage over the stones; moonlight flooded the hills, and the valleys lay in shadow.

"Oh! my love! my love!" thought Allan, in an ecstasy of joy, "I will soon be with you. Will she melt? this grand, stately, Ice Queen? Will she allow me to touch her hand, kiss those rosy lips? Ah! yes! Has she not told me to come? Does it not mean she is to be mine,— all mine? No fear of Cousin Lee any more."

Then he thought of his friend who had striven so honestly for his prize. How he loved her! and, as all accepted suitors can

afford to do, he fell to pitying the poor
fellow who had reached so high and yet
could not touch the fruit.

"She will be my wife,—the marriage
must not be put off," he thought. He
was impatient to get away from his club-
mates now, and settle down among those
"quiet people." What a change had
come over him!

Then he fell to dreaming of their long
honey-moon,—spent in Italy, la belle
France, anywhere she might choose to
wander. He was so absorbed in his love-
dream he did not notice they had entered
the wooded park until they were in sight
of the grand old house. It was lit from
cellar to roof, just as on his first introduc-
tion. The massive hall-doors stood wide
open, and a flood of light streamed out on
the circle of green in front.

Not feeling a moment's uneasiness about
anything, but merely from idle curiosity,
he leaned out of the carriage-windows
and exclaimed,—

" How lighted up you are here to-night,
Uncle Sol !"

" En well we mout be, marster," proudly
replied the faithful old servant.   " I ain't
seen sich a grand marriage 'memorated fur
long time in dese 'ere parts."

" Whose marriage?" said Allan, now
leaning forward to catch every word.

" Ob course, marster, you knows whose
it is,"—and the old negro gave an
amused chuckle,—" 'case you knowed
you cummed up fur ter see Mars' Lee
and Miss Marie git married !"

" Stop ! Stop right here, and put me
out, uncle !" exclaimed Allan, wildly.
Then, remembering himself, he added,
more collectedly, " I'll come to the house
presently."

The old negro had been accustomed to
obey without questioning.   So, calling to
the footman to open the door and pull
down the steps, Allan staggered out, more
dead than alive.

Who was this coming to him through the moonlight?

Was it not his bride-elect?

And this was all a terrible nightmare. He would take the old negro's life for trifling with him, he thought, as hope gave fleetness to his steps.

"Oh, my queen! my Ice Queen! have you come to meet me?" he cried, banishing all his wretched fears in the presence of this beautiful spectre.

It was Marie, robed in white, with a lace shawl thrown lightly over her head; diamonds gleamed in her hair and sparkled on her white throat and rounded arms. She extended her jewelled hands; unshed tears stood in her eyes.

Allan seized her hands and was about to carry them to his lips, when she drew them away quickly, and cried out,—

"Oh, Allan! Allan! I repent, I repent; but it is too late; too late! Come and let me tell you how wicked I have been."

"Tell me first," he said, breathlessly, as he led her to a more retired part of the grounds, and, spreading his handkerchief on the ground, bade her sit there, "that this old negro lied"—great cords stood out on his forehead—"and that you are not to be another's bride."

He stood in front of her with his hands crossed over his breast, as if to steel himself for anything. His serious, stern manner startled the woman at his feet, till, forgetting her pride,—everything,— she exclaimed, wildly,—

"Allan! oh, Allan! pity me! I have ruined your life and—and mine!"

He was touched by her misery, her tears; and, throwing himself on the grass at her side, he said, gently,—

"Tell me all, dearest; go on, I'm prepared for anything—but eternal separation."

Then she told him how she had loved him in her early womanhood; how cruelly he had left her without a word, after

he had forced her to betray her heart's
secret; how her proud heart rebelled at
the unnatural state of affairs, until she
hated him; how Cousin Lee, at this crit-
ical moment, had come and offered his
manly love and been accepted. "And—
and," her voice faltered, but she went on,
"how I longed to see you, just once more.
I thought you were trifling again, and—
you know the rest."

Allan could hardly believe this humbled, crushed girl to be the same proud,
haughty beauty who had turned so coldly
from him in the Quaker City so short a
while ago.

When she had finished, he sprang up
and stood in front of her, still struggling
to control himself for her sake.

"And now! you propose to marry poor
Cousin Lee," he said, sneeringly, "to
wind up this murderous farce."

"I deserve any sneer you may cast
at me. It is the first time in all my life
that I have been so humbled as to be

"'Marie, I swear by heaven'—he raised his hand aloft—'this marriage shall never come to pass!'"

See page 81.

willing to listen to anything you may please to say."

"Then—you shall hear me," he cried, sternly. "You shall know of the wild passions you are trifling with. You are no child now, but a woman; and yet you dare tell me that you love me, and bid me leave you. Marie Washington! a man never loves and leaves the object of his passion in the possession of another without a mighty struggle. You are mine, sweetheart; you belong to me, body and soul! Do you think I will ever give you to another?"

Marie was frightened at his mad words, and, trembling with the intensity of her emotion, exclaimed,—

"Oh, Allan! don't make it so hard for me to do what is right!"

"Marie, I swear by heaven"—he raised his hand aloft—"this marriage shall never come to pass! Fly with me now! I forgive you, darling, but I must have you. Oh, my modest violet! this is the

f

storm that was to throw you into my arms! Come to me! Have we not suffered enough? Could life hold a more cruel hour? The carriage stands at the rack," he urged, seizing her cold hand, as he knelt at her feet; "in a few moments, love, we will be at the dépôt, and in a few hours man and wife! Fly with me, my queen!"

She disengaged her hand, and, springing to her feet, exclaimed, with her old hauteur of manner returning,—

"Allan Cadwallader, you forget the race from which I sprung. They have no histories. Their lives are as placid and as still as this lake stretching out before us. *I* have allowed my wounded pride to lead me into turbulent waters; but I'm not prepared to sacrifice my family, to bring disgrace upon my name, and cruel mortification to the home of my dear aunt and cousin."

"If you fly with me now they will forgive you," he urged, with mad intensity. "In a little while it will all be forgotten. Even Lee would not care to have an unwilling bride. Do not forget how long our lives may be! You could not live out your married life with another, knowing, as you do, that your heart is mine. Marie, is it womanly to deal with Lee so falsely?"

This appeal touched her, but not as he had hoped.

"I know it is all wrong," she said. "I'm going to tell him all to-night, and ask him to forgive and shelter me for the rest of my life; and I will try so hard to love him and make him happy. I have brought all this misery on myself, and must live out its consequences."

"Without a thought or care," exclaimed Allan, angrily, "how the man you love works out his problem. You have made life worthless; do not tempt me to woo death!"

"Miss Marie!" called out Mammy Aggy, "whar is yer? Marse Lee 'most

'stracted 'bout yer. Done nearly walked
de plank out ob de back porch. Chile,
cum on ter de house wid yer ole mammy.
What's de good ob stayin' down here in
de damp air de night befo' ye're married?
Yer gwine ter git sick, sure! Marse
Allan, I hope yer don't think I'm im-
pittent, but I 'clare to God, dis ain't
'zactly rite. Fetch my young mistis ter
de house, ef you please, sah!"

"That's all right. That's all right,
mammy," said Allan, greatly annoyed.
"I'm not going to run off with your
young mistress! I wish to God I
could!" he murmured, as Mammy, having accomplished her errand, returned to
the house.

"Come, wife of my soul!" he cried, in
an agony of persuasion, "in a few hours
we can be man and wife. Let not pride
separate us again! You are the only
woman I ever loved, Marie; come, and
we will be so happy; just think, never
to be parted any more!"

She stood with her eyes cast down, and trembling like a leaf. Allan took heart again.

"Think of my wasted life," he urged, with mad entreaty; "think of the sleepless nights and restless days; think of me as a wanderer on the face of the earth —Noah's weary dove without a mate! Is it true, darling, that you would hold me under the water while Lee jumped into the life-boat at your side? Oh, Marie, my darling, once more—let us fly!"

"We are a proud race, Allan," she said, summoning all her strength to enable her to speak so coolly. "Don't tempt me any further. The God of my mother has helped me to pass the breakers; with His assistance I will steer my boat into safer waters in the future. I am going to ask my last favor, Allan: will you go in, speak to papa and mamma, and I will say that you are obliged to return before —the wedding. Will you give me your arm?"

Her manner was so queenly he dared
not disobey.

"Thank you," she said, quietly, as she
sank heavily on his extended arm, ex-
hausted with the emotional scene she had
passed through.

"Will you forgive me—and forget
me?" she murmured.   "It is best!"

"I will not tell you to forget me," he
cried, bitterly, "for I know it would be a
mockery.   You will be ever haunted by
your soul's mate when you are trying so
hard to be the faithful wife."

She shuddered at his sneering tone.

"I will enter the secret chamber of
your heart and claim you as my own;
one can never banish these spirit-mates.
I will sit with you in your halls of mirth;
hover near you in your hours of ease;
come between you and your wronged husband."

"Hush! hush!" she cried, wildly.   "Do
you want a mad bride to-morrow night,
or are you tempting me to suicide?   Oh,

Allan! have you not punished me enough?"

" Forgive me !"

He halted beneath the shadows of the great trees, and, turning, looked upon the beautiful woman at his side ; his mad passion was fighting against the hardness of his fate.

" But can I not take out with me into the long life of black despair the memory of one kiss ?"

He threw his arm about her waist ; but she drew back in horror.

" Are you mad ?" she cried. " Have you forgotten the nature of the woman you are addressing ? Have I sunk so low that you dare to insult me in my loneliness ?"

His hand fell nerveless at his side.

" Great God ! Forgive me, Marie ; I'm only a man after all ; but take my arm again"—as she drew back—" and you will find me a gentleman. Let's play this farce out," he sneered. " I've yet to congratulate the expectant groom."

They came out of the shadows and entered the parlors. How well they played their part, these men and women of the world !

She entered on his arm, and amid these stately aunts and well-born cousins Miss Washington was herself again. How like her old great-uncle, as, all traces of the storm gone, she pressed forward with courtly dignity to present her friend to her mother.

" How pleased we are to see you again," said Mrs. Washington, her quiet, gentle face beaming with kindly welcome.

" How delighted," said Mr. Washington, pressing his hand cordially, " to have Marie's best friend at her wedding to-morrow."

Neither looked at the other as Allan hastily explained his inability to be present.

"In fact," he added, hurriedly, "I've only come to say, ' how do you do ?' and ' good-by.' I will sail to-morrow for a

prolonged trip abroad, and Uncle Sol
will barely be able to reach the train with
me now."

They were standing under the mar-
riage-bell. Marie drew her arm from his
and stepped aside, with her face as white
as a statue. He turned, looked at her for
a moment, then, glancing up at it, noted
its pure white flowers, much as one would
survey, with rapid glance, the gallows on
which he was to be hung. He actually
commented on its loveliness, and com-
plimented the pretty cousins—who had
pressed up to shake hands—on their work.

Lee could not be found. "He had
wandered out into the grounds," they said.

"How fortunate!" thought Allan : " I
could not carry out the mockery of that
congratulation."

Then, with courtly grace, he extended
his hand to Marie,—she looked another
way,—while he murmured,—

"Thank God, it is over! Now for
oblivion!"

CHAPTER VII.

THE BURIAL OF THE TINY GOD.

SHORTLY after his departure Marie excused herself and retired, without seeing Lee.

"I will tell him in the morning," she thought.

Alone in her chamber; she closed her door, locked and bolted it, a thing she had never done before. Then going to the open casement, she leaned out to cool her aching head.

What were her thoughts,—this scion of a proud race, who dared not do as she willed,—this beautiful woman, about to offer herself "a living sacrifice," to prevent the world from talking?

"I have no letters," she thought, "to burn—he never wrote me *one;* no trinkets to return—he never gave me any.

Only the short, sweet courtship and the terrible farewell to take with me into my new life! Can I ever crush those burning memories out of my heart?"

Then she tried to think of Lee's many noble traits, but Allan stood in the way.

Would she ever hate Lee, she thought, with a shudder. She knew there were wild possibilities in her nature. She might even do that; who knows?

She tried to think what was best for her to do. At last, getting out her writing-desk, she sat down, pen in hand, and wrote out the whole truth to Lee. She told him how, accidentally, as it were, it had all happened; how anxious she was now to make amends in any way; how she could not live the false life presented to her if there were any way out of it, alike honorable to both families; how her heart, as well as his, was broken and her life ruined.

"If you will take me, with my wicked secret, in your keeping," she wrote, "and nurse me back into a love worthy of you, Lee, I'm yours.   I leave everything with you."

She felt relieved when the task was over.

"It should go to him early in the morning," she thought, "and I will await my fate. If he says, in his nobility of soul, as he once did say, 'I do not want you if you do not love me,' then the wedding will not take place," she mused, "and papa and mamma will consider it a great disgrace. The world will say he jilted me. If, on the other hand, he should marry me at all hazards, I *know* I should live to hate him !"

So absorbed was Marie with her unhappy reflections that the morning light stole in at her open window, and still she had made no preparation to retire. She sat with her bare white arms on the window-sill, supporting her aching head.

In a little while she heard some one hastily ascend the steps and knock on

Old Mammy Aggy rushed towards her.

her father's door. A low conversation
ensued. Then the hall seemed to fill
with excited people, and low murmuring
cries reached her ears of "Is he quite
dead?" "Are you sure?" "How terrible!"

"Allan has killed himself!" she wildly
cried, and, rushing towards the door, un-
locked it and stood, clad in her evening
dress, among the grief-stricken family.

They were so affrighted at the deadly
pallor of her face and the wild light in
her eyes that even her mother dare not
break the news to her.

"Who's dead?" she screamed; "who's
dead?"

Old Mammy Aggy rushed towards
her, and, taking her in her arms, cried
out, "Oh, my precious baby, God done
took Mars' Lee away from us. His blessed
will be done!"

Marie fell from her arms in a death-
like swoon, and it was many hours before
they could rouse her.

When she recovered consciousness she begged her mother to tell her all. .

It was a short story.   Lee had always suffered from heart-disease, and the unusual excitement attendant upon his marriage had brought on a fatal termination.

He had been found, early on the morning of his wedding-day, sitting in his chair with her portrait in his hand, quite dead.

CHAPTER VIII.

THE RESURRECTION OF CUPID.

EIGHTEEN months have passed away since the scenes of our last chapter. Marie had put on widow's weeds and given herself up to her music, which she dearly loved. She never heard from Allan. She did not know where he was, or whether he had heard the news of Lee's death at all.

Sometimes her proud nature would rebel at his silence. Sometimes she feared he was dead, or, worse, had learned to love some other woman.

She was devoted to her church-organ, and would often steal away into the silent temple, and pour out her grief in song, accompanied by the melancholy peal of the grand instrument.

One day early in December, when the sun had obscured itself for a while, and the wintry winds were howling around the empty church, blowing the naked branches of the old graveyard trees against the windows and whirling the dead leaves about in piles, Marie seated herself at the organ and was singing, in her clearest, richest tones, "Come, ye Disconsolate," when she heard some one enter the church and walk up the aisle. It was the sexton, perhaps. She did not turn to look; and having finished her hymn, dismissed the organ-boy, and drawing on her gloves, was about to leave the church for her drive home, when she heard a step on the stair which led into the organ-loft. It was a steady, quick step. Did she know it? The lilies were fading and the roses gaining ground in her cheeks. Her soft, brown eyes were filled with a delicious expectancy; every nerve and fibre of her being thrilled with an unspoken hope. A hand was on the door. She could not still the beating of that wild, yearning heart.

It was Allan!

"Oh, my modest violet!" he exclaimed. "I have returned from my wanderings, heard all, and have come to claim my bride!"

He threw his arm about her waist (no resistance now), pressed her to his heart, and kissed her passionately.

"Marie, say you are mine!" he murmured. "Say that nothing shall separate us any more!"

And she whispered, " Yours, till death us do part!"

THE END.

E   g   9